GOODNIGHT EVERYONE

"No dreamer is ever too small, no dream is ever too big."
anonymous

For my sister, Jan, a Montessori teacher,
who inspired the idea for this book

First published 2016 by Walker Books Ltd.
87 Vauxhall Walk, London SE11 5HJ

10 9 8 7 6 5 4 3 2 1

© 2016 Chris Haughton

The right of Chris Haughton to be identified as author/illustrator
of this work has been asserted by him in accordance with the
Copyright, Designs and Patents Act 1988

This book has been typeset in SHH

Printed in China

British Library Cataloguing in Publication Data:
a catalogue record for this book is
available from the British Library

ISBN 978-1-4063-5232-0

www.walker.co.uk

www.chrishaughton.com

WALKER BOOKS
AND SUBSIDIARIES
LONDON · BOSTON · SYDNEY · AUCKLAND

GOODNIGHT EVERYONE

CHRIS HAUGHTON

the sun is going down and everyone is sleepy

the mice

are sleepy

...YAWN

the hares

are sleepy

they sigh

AH.............................

..........YAWN

the deer are sleepy

they take a long, deep breath

AHH..

even

Great

Big Bear

is sleepy

she has a
GREAT, BIG
STRETCH

AHHHH..

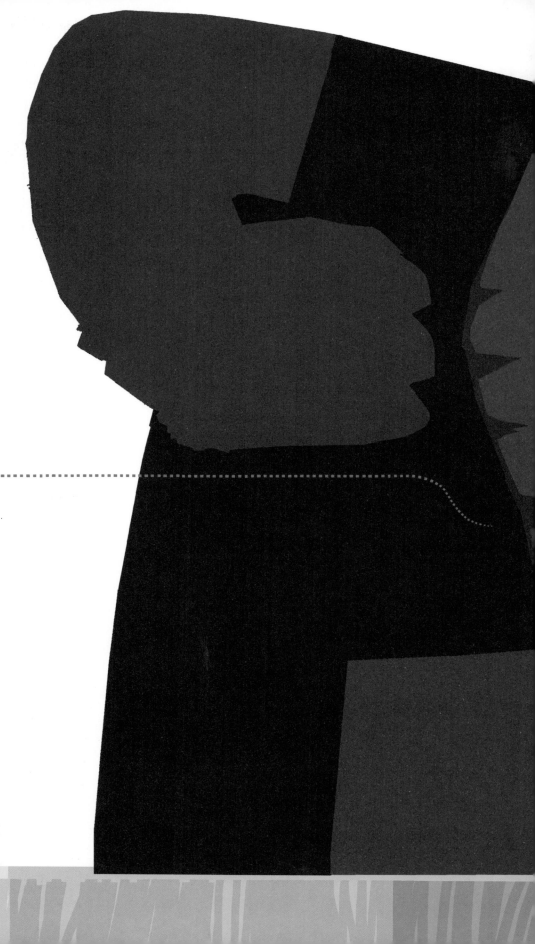

YAWN

"wanna play?" asks Little Bear

"we're too tired"

say the mice

"we're too

tired, too"

say the hares

"aren't you tired?" ask the deer

"oh no, no! not even a little bit"

says Little Bear

but after a
while, Little
Bear sighs

AH.................

takes a
long, deep
breath

AHHHH...............................

and has a

GREAT, BIG,

ENORMOUS

s t r e t c h

AHHHH.........

.............YAWN

"it really must
be time for bed"
says Great
Big Bear

the mice are asleep

they snore

. . . z z Z

and sigh

S S s . . .

goodnight mice

the hares are asleep

...zzzZZZ

SSSss...

goodnight hares

the deer are asleep

...zzZZZZZZ

SSSSSSss...

goodnight deer

Little Bear

gets a great

big goodnight

kiss

:X:

goodnight bears

goodnight everyone

the moon is high and everyone is fast asleep

neptune

uranus

saturn

jupiter

mars

moon

earth

venus

mercury

sun